THE STONE-FACED BOY

The

Stone-Faced Boy

by PAULA FOX

illustrations by Donald A. Mackay

Bradbury Press   Scarsdale, New York

3   75

The text of this book is set in 12 pt. Janson.
The illustrations are pencil drawings, reproduced as halftones.

For Maro, Sasha and Catherine
Chermayeff

chapter 1

Gus was the third child born to the Oliver family. To his surprise, two more arrived after he had.

"The jig-saw puzzle has been completed," Mr. Oliver was fond of saying at the dinner table as he looked at his five children and Mrs. Oliver. If he was a puzzle piece, Gus thought to himself, his outlines were awfully blurred, probably from being squeezed between Rachel who was fourteen and Zachary who was twelve, and Serena who was eight and Simon who was four.

As long as Gus could remember, the Olivers had lived on the slope of a hill in a big wooden house surrounded by neglected apple trees. At the foot of the hill was a narrow bumpy road which led to the village a few miles away where the Oliver children attended school. In the fall, apples rolled down from the orchard and collected in the ditches on either side of the road. In the winter, the snow plow came and exploded the snow into two high banks in which the children sometimes found an old yellow apple frozen into marble. In spring, the ditches filled with lively streams of water that emptied into Currey Pond. In summer, the streams dried up, and black snakes wriggled out from the old stone walls to lie on the road and sun themselves.

On the other side of the road were meadows separated, one from another, by collapsed stone walls. Beyond the meadows rose another line of hills upon whose gentler slopes sat here and there a house not unlike the Olivers'. In the spring mists, the houses looked like large gray birds that had lighted in the clearings. But when it rained, the houses seemed to be growing right up out of the muddy ground.

Nothing special like oats or timothy grass grew in the meadows. No animals grazed in them. That was because the farmers had all gone away and families like the Olivers, who had nothing to do with farming, had moved into the farmers' old houses. Mr.

Oliver, who was an optometrist, drove to his work every day to a town twenty-five miles away. Little farms, Mr. Oliver said, belonged to the past.

When Gus thought about the past—all the time that had gone on before Gus even existed—he imagined that it was all locked into a room on the third floor of his house. Once, when Mrs. Oliver had unlocked the door to get some old photographs, Gus had looked around her and seen what the room contained. Boxes. Trunks. Broken furniture. And in the light from a small round window near the ceiling he saw dust motes floating. They seemed to give off a kind of sound, a kind of low note that midget bees might make. That was the sound of the past, and dust was its smell.

Gus didn't like the third floor at all, mostly because of the blue room across the hall from the storage room. The blue room was empty except for a chair with three legs and a torn cushion spilling out matted lumps of grayish cotton. The walls and the ceiling were painted such a violent color that when Gus peered in he felt the whole room was shrieking at him.

"*Blue!*" it screeched.

There were even drops of blue paint on the window panes and blobs of it on the floor. Like the storage room, the blue room had its own special sound, the noise of its blueness, the drone of wasps and the scrabble of mice inside the plaster, as well as a peculiar kind of stillness in the late afternoon in which Gus could hear the thump of his own heartbeat.

Gus often felt there were too many rooms in the house, too many doors and closets and stair steps and leaking faucets. There were too many animals, curled up in corners, perched on shelves, lurking beneath beds and tables: birds, cats, bugs, mice and a little brown dog named Sheltie who spent most of his time beneath the dining room table eating up all the crumbs the children dropped.

But there were, especially, too many brothers and sisters.

Simon was the worst. He called everybody "dum-dum" and then smashed them with his toy broom. When Simon brought his broom up to firing position, everyone, except Gus, laughed. For reasons Gus couldn't figure out he never ducked in time but always caught the full force of the broom on his head.

Two of Simon's brooms broke on Gus's head. But

then Simon always turned up with a new one he had gotten somewhere. Gus began to think there was a devil who supplied Simon with brooms, a devil who probably lived in the blue room.

Serena was the nicest. She was soft and dreamy and there was nearly always a smile on her face. She could make up games out of anything. She could take a discarded egg box and turn it into a hotel for bugs. She would place a bit of flannel blanket in each little section for a bug rug, and slivers of wood and small round pebbles for bug beds and bug chairs.

When Gus watched her from the door of her room as she sang one of her own songs to herself, kneeling on the floor over the bug hotel, he hoped she would ask him to be part of her game. She never did. It wasn't, Gus knew, because Serena was mean. It was because she was happy by herself.

"Oh, Serena . . ." Gus sighed in his inside voice, but what he said was, "How do you know one of those things won't bite you?" and he pointed at an ant which had either fainted at the luxury of the accommodations or else was dead. Serena smiled up at him and pasted a freshly lettered sign on the top of the box. It read: "Insect Arms."

It was because of Serena that the house was so full of creatures. There were six mayonnaise jars in her room variously occupied by spiders and their egg sacs, caterpillars in their fuzzy hammocks, tiny tree toads belching softly beneath waterlogged leaves, snakes no wider than and as bright green as a blade of spring grass, and once, several small field mice which had died, possibly from being fed too much spaghetti. She especially seemed to like fierce old stray cats which looked as though they'd been attacked by fur-eating moths, and which wailed all night long. Serena made them bibs out of oilcloth and fed them cereal. She had a menu for every animal and every occasion.

Zachary was a thumper and a drummer. He thumped with his feet on the legs of tables, on the side of cartons, on the back of the car seat. He drummed with his fingers on table tops and books and window panes. On weekends, he threw a hard rubber ball up against the walls of the house, dislodging termites and wood dust, and driving Mr. Oliver crazy. Mr. Oliver would send him out to the orchard where Gus could watch him from the living-room window. Zack would throw the ball straight up in the air, grinning as he ran to catch it, scowling when it was deflected by a tree branch. If Zack had absolutely nothing else to do, he would ask Gus to play cards with him. Gus was always glad at first, even though he knew that by the time they were halfway through the game, he would feel terrible.

"Stupid!" Zack would yell as Gus played the wrong card. "Hurry up, creep!" he would grumble when Gus tried to figure out what card he should play.

As for Rachel, she was so old and pretended to be so grown-up that she could hardly bring herself to speak to Gus. Every Saturday morning she made Turkish Delight. When the jellied candy cooled off, she sprinkled a whole box of powdered sugar over it. Every two minutes she stuck a finger into it, "to see if it's ready," as she said. When it was, she allowed each member of the family to have one piece and stuffed herself with the rest. On Saturday afternoons she stayed within a yard of her mirror and rolled up her hair on fat curlers, then let it down, snipped off a lock or two, and rolled it all up again. She liked to startle people. One night, during the chocolate pudding, she said in her shrieky dramatic voice, "The end of the world is coming!"

"Rachel, Rachel . . ." sighed Mrs. Oliver.

7

"That's not news," said Mr. Oliver.

"Ha-ha!" snorted Zack.

"Dum-dum!" screamed Simon.

"We can all hide together under my patchwork quilt," said Serena.

"When?" asked Gus. And then, because it had grown so silent, he added, "When will the end of the world come?" He had just been thinking about the well out in the orchard. When the cistern ran dry, Mr. Oliver carried pails out to the well and filled them with water for cooking and drinking and washing. The well was never dry. Serena wasn't afraid of it. She liked to go out to it in the summer and count the milk snakes that lived near the top among the dark mossy damp stones. But Gus couldn't get within ten feet of it because one night he had dreamed that all the water in all the oceans and the rivers, the lakes and streams and creeks of the world, had poured into the well from under the ground and that all that water was flowing out of the top, covering the orchard, the meadows, the houses, the hills, and all the people and animals and living things.

Gus looked up. Everyone was watching him. Rachel began to smile, then to laugh. "*When*, he said!"

"Cuckoo!" said Zack.

Gus went back to his chocolate pudding and scraped the bowl deliberately. Then he held up his spoon and looked at it closely as if his only concern in the world was to make sure he had not left a drop of pudding on it. At that moment his heart was pounding, for he imagined he could feel the well waters thinly covering the floor beneath the dining table. At the same time, he was aware of every face watching his face, waiting. No one could see that he had lifted both feet off the floor. He dropped the spoon and it clattered in the bowl. He looked up. His eyes met Rachel's eyes. He was sure there was no more expression on his face than there was in the bowl he had just emptied. He touched the floor with one toe. It was dry.

"Stone face!" whispered Rachel.

"Hush!" said Mrs. Oliver.

"Make him stop!" cried Rachel. "Poppa, make him!"

"Leave him alone," Mr. Oliver replied.

Who had first called him "stone face"? Gus wondered. It couldn't have been so long ago. Had he brought the name home from school? Or had he taken it from home?

10

He could hear as though it had just happened Miss Hamilton's voice saying, "Why, Gus, you're not even smiling!" But Miss Hamilton had been his first-grade teacher. And that was four years ago! How *could* he have smiled when the whole room of children were gasping with laughter at him? He had thought over the whole thing a hundred times—his question, Miss Hamilton's smile, the children laughing, the chalk dust rising from the eraser which Miss Hamilton dropped on her desk, the books that fell on the floor as though they too were joining in. And on the board was the round circle of the earth which Miss Hamilton had just drawn and which Gus himself wanted to run up to erase. Four years later, Gus could hear his own question and wish, to this day, that he had never asked it. "How can we see the sky?" he had asked. "How can we see through the earth?"

"But Gus," she had answered, smiling, "we aren't *inside* the earth. We are on the *outside!*"

And he had started to say, "But then why don't we fall off?" when the room exploded with laughter. Later, Billy Carpenter had pushed him up against the chicken-wire fence at the back of the schoolyard and all the boys had teased him. "Inside the earth!" they had shouted mockingly. Was it at that moment he had wiped every expression from his face? And was that why they left him alone finally?

Yet now he felt as if the name had been waiting for him all along, even before he was born. In some ways it was a compliment, although Gus didn't think of it as an especially friendly one. He always won staring matches. His opponent would say, "No one can stare you down, you've got a face made out of stone." Then, too, it made him mysterious because no one knew how he did it. He didn't know himself. It was as though he shut a door. He could even hear the little click of the lock. Right after the click, he knew his face was without expression. Even if Zack shoved him so hard he crashed to the floor, his face was blank when someone turned him over to see if anything was broken.

When he had first noticed how stony his face was getting, he hadn't minded. There were some immediate results. For one thing, Rachel stopped teasing him so much. For another, Zack didn't get as much fun from knocking him about, and when Mr. Oliver said, "You must overcome your fear of the well," Gus didn't even blink. This appeared to discourage Mr. Oliver so that he said nothing further about the subject.

But now Gus had a new kind of trouble. The stone face seemed to have stuck. It stayed with him all the time, when he was in school, even at night when he woke up and listened to the old house creak and groan. He knew that then, when he was so scared, his face wasn't scared. And when he got "A" on an English paper, he didn't smile, and when he got "D" on an arithmetic test, he didn't scowl. When Serena made a hat for a cat, Gus didn't laugh. When the brown custard cups with his favorite dessert in them were brought to the table, he didn't grin. And when his mother buttered slices of bread, holding them in her thin fingers in such a pleasant, appetizing way, he couldn't show the pleasure he felt. What had happened was that he was no longer shutting that little imaginary door. It was shutting itself.

Then, too, people thought he was thinking or doing things he hadn't thought or done. For instance, there was one morning when the children on the school bus got wild and excited and punched each other. The bus driver stopped just outside the village where the school was, and turned around and looked slowly at each child, not saying a word. But when he came to Gus, he said, "What's on your mind, little buddy, eh? How would you like me to report you to the principal? And your Ma and Pa? Eh? And what if there's a blizzard tomorrow morning? You won't be allowed on the bus because you can't behave yourself. We'll just pass you on the road and look out at you, shivering and shaking and cold."

But Gus hadn't done anything! He'd been the only one who hadn't made a sound!

Sometimes he imagined himself as tiny as one of Serena's bugs, running around on the inside of his own head, trying to poke out his mouth so that it would laugh, trying to tickle his eyes so they would cry.

Gus had begun to fear there would come a time, soon, when he couldn't close his eyes to sleep, or open his mouth to eat.

chapter 2

One day in January, a few weeks after the New Year holiday, the school bus had to drop the Oliver children at Currey Pond, half a mile from home, because the snow had piled into drifts during the windy afternoon and the driver was afraid his wheels would get stuck. Simon, of course, did not go to school yet. He would be waiting for them in the kitchen, Gus thought, probably threatening to drop carpet tacks in the cocoa Mrs. Oliver would be fixing for them.

In some places, the snow formed great platters upon which leafless thickets sat. Over the small stream which filled Currey Pond in the summer, snow crusted into thin white roofs that broke when Gus touched them with his boots. Zack was arguing with Serena.

"What do you mean two plus two can make anything? That's so dumb, it makes my ears close up!"

"Two plus two can be anything," Serena said mildly. "What if you added two drops of rain to two drops of rain?"

"Then you'd have four drops of rain," Zack shouted.

"No, you wouldn't," said Serena. "You'd have one big drop."

"Oh, Serena, you're just trying to be different," said Rachel.

"Different from what?" asked Serena. "If you like two and two to be four, it's all right with me."

Zack, in a lightning attack, showered Gus with soft snowballs that scattered all over his wool hat and down the neck of his jacket like cold milkweed. Even when one hit him square on the forehead, his expression didn't change. He looked straight ahead and trudged on.

"Nuts!" said Zack, disgusted. "It'd take an avalanche to make you crack up."

"Wait'll he goes to the dentist next time," Rachel said. "He'll make a face then!"

"The dentist gave me a diamond ring last time," said Serena happily.

"Diamond! It's not a diamond," exclaimed Rachel. "It's just some fake stuff he keeps around for you little kids."

"It's a diamond," said Serena. "I wonder where I put it? Wherever it is though, it's being a diamond right now."

"It's not real, Serena," said Rachel irritably.

"It fits on my middle finger and my finger is real and so the diamond is real," Serena replied. Rachel kicked the snow furiously and Gus wished he could laugh out loud. Serena had caught up with him. He watched her red boots next to his black ones.

"Do you think all the water in the world could come up in our well?" he asked Serena in a low voice so the others wouldn't hear him.

"We'll put the cover on it," she said. It wasn't the answer he'd hoped for, but it would have to do. Serena stopped suddenly and looked out toward the great meadow that sailed right up to the edge of the pine woods which grew along the base of the farthest hills.

"There's a black dog," she said. "It has a white spot on its tail."

Gus was thinking hard about the French knights he had heard of that morning in social studies. Their armor was so heavy they had to be lowered onto their horses with winches.

"There's something wrong with that dog. He's hurt," said Serena. Before anyone could stop her, she ran across the ditch and crawled up over the wall.

"He might bite!" cried Rachel.

"Come *on*, Serena! I want to get home," protested Zack, who realized they would all have to wait for her. It was a law in the family that the youngest could make the oldest wait. Gus supposed, although it seemed unlikely, that once Rachel and Zack had even had to wait for him.

The three of them stood and watched as Serena ran through the heavy snow, her red woolen scarf sliding down her back and trailing behind her. The dog, which was lying in the snow, didn't wag its tail or even look up as Serena came near it. Gus felt a sudden chill that was not from the cold. Perhaps the dog was mad! Perhaps it was not even a dog but a wolf! Hadn't his father said that some hunter had spotted a pack of gray wolves last winter? He wondered if he should take a chance and ask Rachel if there were black wolves. But it didn't come out as a question.

18

"There are black wolves," he said.

"There are not," Rachel said.

"That's just some old farm dog that's been out chasing snowshoe rabbits," said Zack.

Serena had reached the animal and was bending over it. The dog rose very slowly as though its legs were rusty pliers. Even from this distance it was possible for Gus to see that Serena was talking to the dog, and that its head was bent forward as if it were listening to her.

"She's got it to follow her," said Rachel.

"It's bigger than she is," Zack observed.

"Funny looking. Just what Serena likes," said Rachel.

What, Gus wondered, had Serena said to the dog to make it get up and come with her? But that was not the right question. Animals didn't understand words. Gus knew that. It was something special about Serena herself that animals recognized. He couldn't think what it was. Perhaps they recognized something about him, too. Perhaps that's why they barked at him or yowled or hissed or stung him. He couldn't remember a summer when he hadn't been chased by paper wasps, growled at by dogs who spotted him

from half a mile away, sprung upon from behind a bush by some crazy old cat.

"He's got sore feet," Serena called out. "And old summer burrs in his fur that nobody took out. His nose is scratched and he's a mess."

She began to shove the dog over the stone wall. The dog looked exhausted but not in the least upset by Serena's effort to move it. Then it caught sight of Gus. The dog growled. Its fur rippled and its ears rose.

"I'll go ahead," muttered Gus, feeling like a plague but relieved to put distance between himself and the dog. No one tried to stop him. Zack and Rachel went up the side of the ditch and hauled on the dog's paws until, at last, he slid over the wall and fell into a heap in the ditch.

As Gus walked on, he comforted himself with the thought that Sheltie didn't growl at him. He simply ignored him. But that might be, Gus thought, because Sheltie had gotten so fat from living underneath the dining-room table that there was no room left in him for a growl.

There was a strange look about the sky, a very faint pinkness at the edge of the gray. There were rare days like this in January when Gus felt he could almost choose the kind of weather he wanted for the next day; he could say, 'Make it summer tomorrow morning,' or 'Let's have a real blizzard, let the snow fall and cover the orchard, the old unused barns, the splintery gray slats of the empty chicken coops, the pond, the houses, the hills and the well. Let the snow fill up the well like tobacco fills up the bowl of Poppa's pipe.' He would certainly choose the blizzard.

Just ahead and up on the slope was home. The light that came through the kitchen windows fell on the snow. It was reddish and warm-looking, as though it were already evening instead of late afternoon. When Gus looked up at the sky, just before running along the drive to the house, he saw that the pink had now disappeared and that darkness was beginning to flow over the eastern hills.

As he ran, his boots crunching and squeaking on the snow, he felt that wave of happiness which always seemed to be waiting for him at this spot on the hill as though it were a person rushing out to greet him. Then he imagined the mug of hot cocoa and the buttery toast that would be waiting for him inside on the kitchen table. He thought of all the familiar smells and noises of the house, of dropping his school books with a great bang! on the floor, the thawing of the tip of his nose and his ear lobes and frozen finger tips which had pushed through the ends of the old woolen mittens he was wearing. He saw himself racing up to his room which, even though Rachel had said it looked as if he shared it with sea-gulls, was *his* room.

This very moment, Gus wanted to laugh out loud, at least to grin. He took one hand from a mitten and ran it over his face. "*Grin!*" he ordered himself. But he could not.

What *was* he going to do? Pretty soon he would have to start carrying around signs—signs that read: *laughter; scowling; puzzlement; curiosity; anger—* which he would have to hold up over his head, like the people in a parade who carried banners.

The happiness left him.

Then he noticed the car parked in front of the back door. And what a car! He'd never seen one like it. It was as red as a fire engine. It had a long snout. Gus peered at the dashboard, which was like an airplane's.

He looked quickly through the kitchen window.

A very large woman was sitting at the table. Standing at her knee, looking up at her and speaking animatedly, was Simon. The woman was smoking a small black cigar. Suddenly she removed it with a flourish from her mouth, and said something to Simon. He dropped instantly out of sight. Gus looked down through the window. Simon was on the floor, rolling around and laughing. Mrs. Oliver appeared, carrying a cup and saucer which she set down in front of the woman. Then the woman reached down, picked up Simon by his sweater collar, shook him and set him upright. Simon looked astonished.

The woman had bright yellow hair tightly wound around her head like a piece of cloth. She was wearing thick wintry-looking clothes. She looked, thought Gus, like a pile of tweed with a grapefruit stuck on the top.

He tried to open the back door. As usual, it resisted until he put his shoulder against it, shoved and half fell into the summer kitchen, where the air was a little warmer than outside but still damp, and full of the smell of musty apples. On a shelf in a corner, winking in the gray light like cats' eyes, were the glass jars of preserves and jellies his mother had made last summer. There were rubber boots all over the floor and not one matched another. There were sleds leaning up against the wall, and rakes and shovels and pails and all the other things no one knew where else to put. He opened the door to the kitchen.

"Here's Gus," said Mrs. Oliver. "But where are the others?"

"Serena found a dog and they had to drag it over the stone wall," Gus replied.

"Not another animal!"

"He's big, five times bigger than Sheltie," said Gus, wondering why he was exaggerating so.

"He is not," said Simon.

"You don't know what five times anything is," said Gus.

"Why didn't you wait for your brother and sisters?" asked Mrs. Oliver in her in-front-of-company voice.

"The dog didn't like me," Gus answered.

Simon giggled. "It would like me," he said.

"You are wicked," said the yellow-haired woman to Simon.

Simon, who was holding his broom, got that peculiar look on his face which meant he was going to swat someone.

"If you hit me with that broom, I'll break it over

your skull," said the woman. Mrs. Oliver laughed nervously.

"Oh, he doesn't mean it," she said.

"Yes, he does," said the woman, contradicting Mrs. Oliver entirely but without quite sounding rude. "And so do I."

Simon began to sweep up some imaginary dust near the woman's feet.

"Be careful of my crocodile shoes," she said. "They might take a bite out of your broom. They are partial to brooms."

Simon's mouth opened to answer, but then to Gus's surprise he said nothing.

"What kind of a car is that?" Gus asked, feeling he would like to drop his school books but not sure he ought to.

"That," said the woman, "is a Stutz Bearcat. It was built in 1926. Since things always go from bad to worse, they're not making cars that good any more."

"This is your Great-aunt Hattie," said Mrs. Oliver, looking watchfully at Simon who was staring at Great-aunt Hattie's cigar.

"Girls don't smoke cigars," Simon announced.

"That's what you think," said Great-aunt Hattie.

"There are more things in heaven and earth than you've dreamt of, Horatio."

"Horatio!" shouted Simon.

"Your father's aunt," Mrs. Oliver continued as though in a daze. "She has come to stay with us tonight. Isn't that nice?"

When someone says *Isn't-that-nice?* the answer, Gus thought, is always no. But his great-aunt was so odd that in her case the answer might be *perhaps*. She didn't appear afraid of Simon and that alone distinguished her from most adults. When Gus thought of Simon going to school next year, he could imagine the teachers running out the door and jumping out of windows. Although Simon only came up to Gus's waist, Gus had the impression sometimes that he was growing so fast, he and his broom, that in a year he would be three times as tall as he was now.

Great-aunt Hattie was bending over and peering into an enormous blue pocketbook that lay upon her feet like a faithful dog. "Ah!" she said and took from it a small silver flask, uncapped it and poured a brownish-looking liquid into her coffee.

"Yes," Mrs. Oliver said, as though answering a question. "Yes. She's come all the way from Italy just

27

to see her grand-nieces and grand-nephews whom she's never seen before. Imagine!"

"This coffee is ghastly," said Great-aunt Hattie. "I will send you an expresso machine upon my return. If you continue to drink this scree you'll all turn into dwarfs."

"What did you put in your cup?" Simon asked. Great-aunt Hattie looked at him for a long time. Her eyes were round and blue and her skin was wrinkled yet soft looking like one of Mr. Oliver's old leather gloves.

"Poison," Great-aunt Hattie answered at last.

chapter 3

"I like rooms with large windows," Great-aunt Hattie was saying, "windows that reach from ceiling to floor. I like doors which open wide to the outdoors. I like marble floors and ceilings that look like white frosted wedding cakes, but not clutter. I hate clutter. I like my little Italian palazzo because when I open a window there, the sky comes right into the room."

"What about the rain?" asked Zack, who was about to bite into a piece of almond cake baked especially in Great-aunt Hattie's honor. "Does the rain come in too?"

"The rain must be restrained," said Great-aunt Hattie sternly. "But it seldom rains where I live. The sun shines down on water the color of turquoise, and rays of light ring the masts of ships that lie in the harbor just below my windows. Beyond the ships rises the beautiful triangle of a still-active volcano."

"Could it blow up?" asked Rachel excitedly.

"At any time," replied Great-aunt Hattie.

"I'm afraid we can't offer you such a view here," said Mr. Oliver. "But we'll give you Gus's room. That is, at least, near the stairs which lead to the front door."

"That will do," said Great-aunt Hattie, opening up her little silver flask and pouring a drop of whatever it was into her coffee.

His room! Gus stood up from the dining table.

"Going to clean your room?" asked Rachel slyly.

Unable to speak, Gus nodded.

"Poppa will set up that nice little camp cot for you," Mrs. Oliver said, looking faintly worried. "In the blue room."

Gus swallowed a lump of almond cake.

Serena said, "I'll help you clean up."

Gus shook his head. "No thanks," he mumbled, the cake sticking in his throat.

"Sweep everything into the closet," advised Great-aunt Hattie.

Gus had gotten as far as the summer kitchen when

he realized it was too cold outside to run away, he didn't have a suitcase of his own, and he might stumble into the well in the darkness of the orchard. Perhaps he could persuade Sheltie to come to the blue room with him. How could he possibly spend a whole night in there by himself?

Something was growling at him from the summer kitchen. It was Serena's new dog and it must have sensed Gus was there even though it was behind a closed door.

Miserable, Gus wandered off to the little back parlor. He was so worried about sleeping in the blue room that he forgot to turn on the table lamp the right way so that he got a little electric shock. His fingers tingling, he turned to the television set. The sound had gone months ago. Now when the children watched a program, Serena made up speeches for the actors and announcers. Gus turned on the set. Little droplets of light dripped across the gray surface of the picture tube. Suddenly a huge pack of dogs emerged from the fog. A dish of food was set before them by a human hand. They began eating. A man with wavy hair was flashed onto the screen. He was smiling and talking and pointing at the dogs.

"The man is saying that the dogs have stolen his

food," said Serena, who had just come into the parlor.

"Then why is he smiling?" asked Gus, despite himself. He didn't really want to have a conversation with Serena at the moment.

"He has to smile because he has so many extra teeth," said Serena. "If he ever stops smiling, he'll bite himself."

"Oh, Serena!" exclaimed Rachel who had just followed Zack into the room. Rachel began to fiddle with the channel selector.

"Why does she have to have my room?" Gus asked.

"She needs to make a quick getaway," replied Zack.

"Your room is convenient," added Rachel smugly, thinking, Gus was sure, of her horrible pink curlers which she wouldn't have to put away in a box where they belonged.

"Rachel, leave that one on," said Zack.

"I hate cowboys," Rachel said.

"I have to do my homework," announced Serena.

"Oh, you don't have any homework," cried Rachel. "You're just showing off!"

"I'm going to finish taking the burrs out of my dog," said Serena calmly. "Any work I do at home is homework."

"That dog is so old it needs a cane to walk with," said Zack.

"I've decided to call him Tipper," said Serena.

"You'd better call him Father Time," Rachel said.

Gus couldn't bear any of them right now. It wasn't that they were fighting. That was occasionally interesting when he wasn't involved. But when they wrangled like this he was reminded of small unpleasant things like belts that were too big, or Zack's hand-me-down shirts with the cuffs that drooped over his knuckles or cranky Sunday afternoons when no one had a thing to do. There was always the danger, too, that Zack and Rachel would gang up on him.

"How old is Great-aunt Harriet?" asked Serena.

"She must be very old if she's Poppa's aunt," Zack said.

"She doesn't look so old. She doesn't look any age," said Serena.

"What's the stuff she pours out of that silver bottle?" asked Rachel. "I'd like to taste it."

"Why don't you?" suggested Gus. "She told Simon it was poison."

"She didn't!" exclaimed Rachel.

"It's stewed cigars," said Zack.

"Uff!" snorted Rachel, making a disgusted face. "I think it's rum."

"It's something to make her shrink so she can get through doors," said Serena.

Mr. Oliver ran suddenly into the room. He looked back quickly over his shoulder.

"Now, children . . ." he began. "Rachel, leave that channel switch alone. Now listen, children. I expect you to behave yourselves with Great-aunt Harriet, even if she is strange and not what you'd expect. I think she's goodhearted. Let's hope so. And she's only here for one night. Gus, why aren't you cleaning up your room? Rachel and Zack, go clear off the table. Serena, what *are* we going to do about that old dog you found?"

"Poppa, he's not so old," Serena said. "Middle-aged maybe."

"But we have a dog," said Mr. Oliver, "and mice, spiders, snakes, cats and five children."

"Sheltie isn't a dog," said Zack. "He's just a pillow with a dog's stomach."

"I'll go get Tipper," said Serena.

"Did Great-aunt Hattie ever visit you when you were little?" Rachel asked her father.

"Never," he replied unhesitatingly. "The only time I remember seeing her is when she sailed away to Italy and we all went down to the dock to see her off. I must have been around ten, your age, Gus. I was not, I suppose, much interested in aunts. There was a wonderful red-striped canopy over the gang-plank and there was a little band that sat on the top deck and played, 'Toot, Toot, Tootsie, Goodbye,' and hundreds of people leaning on the railings looking down on all of us who were staying home. Someone said, 'Look up and wave' and someone else pointed her out. She didn't believe in waving and the ship was so huge, the crowd so great, that people's faces looked like the buttons in your mother's button box."

"And you never saw her except that once?" asked Rachel.

"Just that once," said Mr. Oliver.

"But then, how did she know where to find you?" asked Zack.

"I just don't know," Mr. Oliver said in a puzzled voice.

"Maybe," said Rachel breathlessly, "she isn't Great-aunt Harriet at all! Maybe there *isn't* any Great-aunt Harriet!"

There followed a long pause during which Mr. Oliver looked from one child to another, and each child looked back at him. A gray peacock appeared on the television screen and silently spread its tail feathers.

"Impossible," said Mr. Oliver, at last.

"My best friend, Meg, told me her mother gave a tea party and a little old white-haired lady came and ate up all the cranberry muffins and had six cups of tea, and when she left it turned out that nobody knew who she was," said Rachel.

"No, no . . ." said Mr. Oliver. "This is different."

Serena came back with Tipper padding after her. "He ate a box of cornflakes," she said.

"But if you haven't heard from Great-aunt Hattie all these years, or heard anything about her—" Rachel began.

"It's out of the question!" said Mr. Oliver in an agitated voice. "Simply not possible. I'm *sure* I had an Aunt Harriet. Of course I did! My father's elder sister."

"You're not sure!" Rachel said triumphantly.

"Don't be disagreeable, Rachel," said Mr. Oliver sharply.

"Did she bring that car all the way from Italy?" asked Zack. "That's the worst looking car I ever saw. It's older than Serena's dog."

"But . . ." Mr. Oliver continued, staring at the television screen on which one man was breaking a chair on another man's head, "was Harriet her name? Or was it Bridget? Aunt Bridget? Or Mary? Or Phillippa?" He looked exasperated. "Why can't I remember? But then I only saw her when she was sailing away. And after all, who else could she be?"

"Why couldn't she have Simon's room?" asked Gus, knowing that his face was at its stoniest, as it always was when he wanted something.

"Good heavens, Gus!" exclaimed Mr. Oliver. "Where's your spirit of adventure? When I was your age there was nothing I liked better than sleeping in a room that wasn't my own."

The television set was turning into a big wad of gray bubble gum. Oh, thought Gus, if he could only throw himself on the floor and roll around the way Simon did when he was angry. If only he could squeeze out a few big tears the way Rachel did when she was begging for something she couldn't have! If he could only scowl and shout the way Zack did when he had to do something he didn't want to do!

How he dreaded sleeping in that blue room! He was sure this was one of those occasions when it wouldn't have mattered even if he had rolled on the floor or cried or shouted and scowled, but at least, if he could have done any of those things, people would know how he felt.

Rachel twiddled with the set again, Zack thumped a chair leg with his foot, Serena buried her hand in the scruffy fur of Tipper's mane. His father looked pensively at the floor.

Great-aunt Hattie appeared in the doorway smoking one of her cigars. She looked suspiciously at the door frame.

"Look how they build these modern houses," she said. "There's hardly room for a worm to crawl through here."

"This is a two-hundred-year-old farm house," said Mr. Oliver. "We have always found the doorways adequate." He sounded quite formal.

"Modern is a relative term," replied Great-aunt Hattie. She blew out a thin coil of cigar smoke which shot across the room and curled up over the television set like a small snake-shaped cloud.

Gus took a step back. There was a long low growl near his heels. He looked down. Serena was pulling a burr from the base of one of Tipper's ears. The dog was looking straight up at Gus.

"Dog doesn't care for you, does he?" observed Great-aunt Harriet.

"I don't care," said Gus.

Mr. Oliver said he must fix the camp cot, and Zack and Rachel went off to clear the table. Great-aunt Hattie managed, by edging sideways, to get into the parlor. Gus saw that Simon was just behind her, holding the large blue pocketbook.

"Put my bag down on that chair," ordered Great-aunt Hattie. Obediently, Simon put the pocketbook down on the chair she had indicated, then looked up at her expectantly. "Don't interrupt," said Great-aunt Hattie. Simon giggled. "Don't giggle either," she said. Simon looked solemn at once. She turned her attention to Gus who began to feel even more uncomfortable than he usually did when someone's attention lighted on him. Serena was singing softly to the dog as she brushed its fur with a doll's hairbrush.

"What do you mean, you don't care?" asked Great-aunt Hattie.

Gus shrugged.

"That is a poor answer. Out of all the thousands of answers you might have given, 'I don't care' is by far the worst choice. And a shrug like that is even worse. The only time you should use such a shrug is when you are bargaining for a piece of Venetian glass and you want to indicate to the shopkeeper that the price he is asking is ridiculous. Simon, fetch me my bag."

After Simon handed it to her, she opened it and looked inside. She rummaged around, then took out a stone, held it up to the light, then thrust it at Gus.

"Take it," she said. "It's a gift."

Gus took it. It looked like a perfectly ordinary gray stone, the kind one could find among the roots of the apple trees, or on the edge of the driveway, or in the schoolyard.

"Hold it up to the light," ordered Great-aunt Hattie.

Gus held it up, turned it, then noticed a crack in the surface.

"Look inside that crack," said Great-aunt Hattie.

Gus squinted and brought the stone close to his

eyes. He was startled to see a faint shimmering, a faint glow as though inside the stone there was a tiny but intense light.

"Do you know what that is?" asked Great-aunt Hattie.

"No," Gus answered.

"It is called a geode," she said.

"Say 'thank you' Gus," murmured Mrs. Oliver who happened to be passing the parlor at that moment, carrying fresh sheets and a blanket.

"Thank you," said Gus.

"Never mind that," muttered Great-aunt Hattie. "Gus, don't you want to know what a geode is?" She didn't wait for an answer but went right on. "It is a hollow stone, you see, and it is lined with crystals. The crystals account for the gleam. They are considered great finds. In one sense, you might say a geode is an accident, even if a splendid one. The stone must have a crack; it must be in a special place where minerals seep into it, certain kinds of minerals. So, in another sense, it is not an accident at all. . . . Think what you like about it, in fact."

Was she waiting for him to answer? Gus wondered. But, in view of all the information she had

42

given him, he could think of nothing to add. So he thanked her again.

"What are you going to give me?" asked Simon hopefully.

"The pleasure of my company," said the old lady, and she gave an unexpected shout of laughter.

chapter 4

Gus supposed Rachel was right. It was probably babyish to take all those things up to the blue room—the stuffed armadillo, the miniature Turkish scimitar and the box of plastic candy he had fooled the whole fifth grade with last September.

She had punched open his door on her way to bed and seen the little collection he had heaped up on his pajamas.

"Well!" she had cried. "If that isn't the silliest—where do you think you're going anyhow? Saskatoon?"

So Gus put everything back on his shelf. He took, instead, a book on the history of the Erie Canal that someone had given him two Christmases ago, and he slipped the geode into the toe of one of his slippers. He didn't know why he paid any attention to what Rachel said. Her brains must be dented by now from the continuing pressure of those curlers.

"My snake got out," announced Serena casually as she passed his door. Mrs. Oliver hurried after her, looking stunned. She didn't care for snakes. Then Zack, tossing a doughnut up in the air, padded by, saying, "It's your turn to wake us tomorrow, Gus. And don't try to get out of it."

All the children tried to get out of it, because the alarm clock had a peculiar double tick, very loud, that kept you awake all night unless you covered it up with a blanket. But if you covered it with a blanket, you had to sit up practically the whole night for fear you wouldn't hear the alarm when it went off.

Sheltie ran by, his nose close to the worn old green carpet.

Simon, wearing his pajamas with feet and riding his broom like a horse, cantered past.

Mr. Oliver looked in, then gave Gus the alarm clock. It was ticking away like a bomb.

"Put your sneakers in the closet," he said. "Great-aunt Harriet might trip over them."

Then Tipper came and stood just outside the door-way. He sniffed the air; his eyes rolled around in their sockets like an angry cow's. Then he sat down on his haunches and proceeded to watch Gus. Gus felt embarrassed. It was dreadful to be watched by a dog. "Go away!" he whispered. Tipper growled. Gus's neck prickled. He went into his closet. He wished that his door was a big television screen so that when someone, or something, he didn't care to see was standing there in front of his room he could switch to a different channel.

"Wow!" he said suddenly and shivered a little. There was something in his baseball cap in a corner of the closet. It was Serena's snake, curled up and apparently asleep. He lifted it out and it dangled from his hand like a shoestring. Then he backed out of his closet. Tipper was gone. In his place stood Great-aunt Hattie.

"Thank you for giving up your room," she said in a kindly voice he had not yet heard her use. "It's always somewhat disagreeable to have to make way for a visitor. What are you holding in your hand?"

Gus felt shy and could think of nothing to say. The snake climbed the air as though there were a small if invisible hill in it, then drooped down again.

From the end of the hall came Mr. Oliver's shout, "Wash your teeth!"

"That snake hasn't much energy," Great-aunt Hattie remarked in her usual tone. "It looks like a worn-out rubber band. Probably sleeps too much. Sleep is a waste of time. I'm glad to see you have a reading light. I shall drop off for an hour before dawn, but until then I will read and think."

Gus stood silently near the door, waiting for her to enter so he could leave.

"It's very difficult to maintain a blank face, to neither smile nor scowl," she said, and walked into the room. "Your brother, Simon, has a similar problem, although he manages it differently. He makes so many faces it is hard to tell what he looks like. That's the loudest alarm clock I have ever heard. You'd do better to keep a rooster in the room."

Gus slipped into the hall. "Goodnight," he said quickly over his shoulder. But Great-aunt Hattie didn't answer.

He went by Serena's room and dropped the snake on the floor. It instantly wriggled through the crack beneath the door.

"Why, *there* you are!" he heard Serena exclaim delightedly.

There was a night light burning in the hall. The stairs leading up to the third floor were dark, but Gus could make out a faint glow on the upper landing. There must be a light on somewhere up there.

Sheltie was curled up on Mr. Oliver's old army blanket at the end of the hall near the radiator. Gus picked him up, blanket and all, and Sheltie snuffled once or twice but didn't open his eyes. As Gus climbed the stairs he heard all the going-to-bed sounds in the house. He felt sad as though he'd been forgotten and locked outside for the night.

In her room, Serena was singing. Rachel was dropping things. Zack was kicking the broken old punching bag that he kept on the floor of his room where it rolled around like a hedgehog. Simon was jumping up and down on his trundle bed, but any second now he would take the highest jump of all, then collapse on the blanket and fall off to sleep instantly. Mr. and Mrs. Oliver were speaking together in low voices. Tipper must be somewhere too, beneath a sofa or a table wherever Serena had decided to make a bed for him.

Where had the dog come from? Gus wondered

as he climbed the last step. But no one would ever know, he thought. Animals couldn't tell you about themselves.

How quiet the third floor was! Even during the daytime it was still up here, but the darkness sealed in the silence so that it felt like the inside of a thick drift of snow, or the way water feels when you swim beneath the surface. The door to the blue room was open and Gus saw the camp cot with a brown blanket flung over it, almost covering its crossed stick legs. Either his father or his mother had put a little lamp on a stool near the cot. The blue of the walls and ceilings looked almost black until he got inside the room.

He deposited Sheltie and his blanket beside the cot, then looked around for a place to put the alarm clock. The broken chair had been pushed into a corner but the torn cushion was in the same old place, lumps of grayish cotton all around it. Gus stuck the clock as far inside the cushion as he could. Then he saw what he had never noticed in the daytime, a crack that meandered all over the wall facing the cot. The thin white line suggested a continent, but not one he had ever seen in his geography book. Perhaps the lost continent of Atlantis would look like that if it ever emerged from the sea which had buried it. He would be the first human on its shore. The animals would be friendly; none would growl at him. The birds would light on his shoulders and he would wear the wasps like rings on his fingers. At night he would lie down to sleep with a llama on either side to keep him warm. The streams would all be shallow, a light clear greenish blue, and there would be no deep holes from which water could pour out and drown everything.

Ah . . . it was only a crack in a blue wall, not a continent. There was no such place; no such wasps, no such llamas. He looked at the windows and saw a blur which must be his own reflection. Perhaps the trouble with him was that he had swallowed a small extraordinary animal which in turn had swallowed up all his expressions, his tears, the sounds of laughing.

Right this minute he was scared to death! The house was silent. He was alone in the special way one is when everybody else is asleep. Yet he could not frown or cry or do anything at all but feel a deep shiver in the very center of himself as he thought of the long night ahead.

The Stone-Faced Boy

He thought suddenly of what Great-aunt Hattie had said, that it was difficult to maintain a blank face. You maintained a pony by feeding it and making it comfortable. How did you maintain a face? And, he wasn't in the least like Simon! The very idea distressed him. Usually when someone described something you were doing as "difficult," it was a compliment. But Great-aunt Hattie hadn't sounded as if she was praising him. She had guessed something private about him, something that was different from the usual comments that everyone in the Oliver family and his teachers and classmates made. He hadn't thought anyone would know that he was *trying* to keep from smiling or frowning. Perhaps though, she didn't know that he also had the opposite problem of trying to make his face show *something*. Oh, why couldn't things be like they used to be?

Cautiously, he tiptoed to the windows. It was not as black outside as he had thought it would be. The orchard was in deep shadow but lakes of moonlight lay on the meadows. The trees were unmoving, so still they might have been painted with a black crayon. The road to the village, so familiar during the day, like a passageway in a house, was mysterious now, its snow-covered length unwinding beneath trees, then emerging like a chalk line drawn on black paper, then curling around a hill and disappearing. Quite clearly, as though it were right outside the windows, he could see the field stones in an old wall that marked off a neighboring meadow. The moon sailed just along the rim of a mass of dark thick clouds. The hills, the mountains beyond them, seemed to Gus to be rolling away like waves. He could not make out the well in the apple orchard, and he was not sorry. Even to think of it made him feel uneasy.

He went to the cot, picked up his book on the Erie Canal and kicked off his slippers. The geode rolled out on the floor. What an ordinary little stone it was! He picked it up and turned it over in his hand. Still, it wasn't absolutely ordinary. There was that little crack, that strange white radiance somewhere inside it. He sighed. Great-aunt Hattie was certainly an odd old lady. He wondered what else she carried in that big blue pocketbook.

The cot was somewhat like a hammock but not nearly as comfortable. He wriggled down into it and began to read. In 1825, a barrel of Lake Erie water was emptied into the Atlantic Ocean, then the Canal was opened. It was once called "Clinton's Ditch" after Governor De Witt Clinton. Gus wouldn't have minded seeing them pour the barrel of water into the ocean, but he didn't find much else interesting.

Sheltie whimpered. Gus sat up straight and the book fell off his lap and onto the floor with a bang. Sheltie's eyes were closed; one leg twitched as though he were dreaming that he was running.

Gus picked up the book but didn't open it. There was no more moonlight and the windows were as black as tar. He would have liked to have gotten up, gone across the room and looked out the windows, but at the moment he was afraid to move at all, afraid even to lie back on his pillow. The whole room seemed to be breathing with him.

"Sheltie," whispered Gus.

Sheltie groaned.

"Oh, wake up, you awful dog!" he pleaded in a low voice.

Sheltie's lids quivered, then raised barely enough for Gus to see the whites of his eyes.

Something scrabbled behind the wall. There was a distant clack-clack as of bare branches striking each other. Had a wind come up? Was it blowing across the empty snow-covered meadows?

His father had said the house was two hundred

years old. Until then, Gus had never thought that the house had been standing so long before he was born, even before his father was born. Someone had once had this room, looked out those windows at the hills. Someone who had lived two hundred years ago.

The house creaked and groaned. Sheltie snored. Why not take the blanket and go downstairs to the living room and sleep on the couch? The very thought of it made Gus feel so much better that he stopped listening to his own breathing. But then he imagined everyone's comments when they found him down there in the morning. Of course, he could set the alarm clock an hour earlier. Then no one would know where he had spent the night. But that wouldn't work either. No matter what time the alarm went off, Simon was always up and about long before. Simon would find him in the living room and shout out the news to everyone in the house.

What was that? A thud, a door banging, footsteps. Gus dived under the blanket, his heart pounding, his eyes squeezed shut. The minutes passed. Everything grew quiet again. Gus, still dizzy with fear, realized he had forgotten to take off his socks, as usual. It made his mother so annoyed. "Oh, Gus!" she would say. How he wished she would come up to the blue room and say it right now!

He slowly pulled the blanket from his face and imagined himself walking down the stairs, going to his parents' bedroom, touching his mother lightly on the shoulder the way he used to do long ago. He imagined her waking suddenly with a little sigh the way she always did and saying, "Yes? Gus? or is it Zack? Or is it Rachel? Oh, dear. I'm so sleepy!"

And then she would get up and take him back to his room and sit with him until whatever it was that had been bothering him had gone away. Sometimes, even late at night, she made him a little special glass of something—orange juice, or milk with a table-spoon of honey in it.

But that was years ago. Everything he liked seemed to have happened years ago.

Was this the longest night of the year? Wasn't it sometime in January? It would be just his luck to get stuck up here on the longest night, Gus thought. His eyes felt itchy. He yawned. Sheltie stretched out with a three-note groan. How strange it was in a house when everyone was sleeping—as though they had all gone away. Sleep took you to some place you couldn't remember later on when you woke up and got dressed and rubbed your face with a little handful of cold water and ran downstairs and had breakfast and everybody talked and ate and got ready for the day. But no one ever mentioned that they had all been away for hours and hours.

He let his arm dangle over the side of the cot. It touched Sheltie's paw. He held the paw and his eyes gradually closed. But he was not quite asleep. There, behind his closed lids, little bright colored dots swam like fish in a tank. That was probably because he had left the light on. But it was better that way. The dark in the blue room would be like a wave covering his head, drowning him.

He had a sudden impression that someone was standing next to the cot, looking down at him silently. He refused to open his eyes. In fact, he was so sleepy, he couldn't open his eyes.

If it was a ghost who lived in the blue room—not that he believed in ghosts—but if it was, then there was nothing he could do anyhow. The ghost would lift him up and carry him behind the blue walls where bells as large as houses chimed each second, where each vibration had a visible shape, like a spark struck off metal by a hammer.

The vibrations of the bells would fill the air with

flying things like strange birds, but all else behind the walls would be still, silent, unmoving, stones shaped like trees and animals, even a river of stones, rolling without sound down to a sea of rock.

With a start, with a violent flinging off of the brown blanket, he sat straight up. A great baying sound was flooding the room. Sheltie was on his feet, his tail straight out, his eyes wide open. Then the baying stopped, only to begin again further away, then stopped, then started once again until it was at last only a faint faraway sound, an echo. Then Gus heard the soft sound of slippered feet on the stairs coming up to the third floor.

He was too scared to look at the door. Instead he watched Sheltie's stiffly turning head as Sheltie moved around to face the door.

It was Serena, a blanket draped around her shoulders, standing in the doorway and crying.

chapter 5

"Tipper's run away," she sobbed. "And he's got caught in a trap. He wanted to go outside so I went down and let him out the back door. He ran right off, through the orchard. I waited and waited but he didn't come back. Now he's trapped somewhere and can't get loose." She wiped her eyes with the edge of the blanket.

"How do you know he's in a trap?" Gus asked, not as sorry for the straying Tipper as he was glad for Serena's unexpected company.

"I heard him crying," she said.

"We can go look in the morning before school," Gus said. He was watching the tears run down Serena's cheeks, and he was secretly amazed. He couldn't remember that he had ever seen her cry before. But she must have cried when she was a baby. All babies cried. Yet he couldn't recall even that.

"He'll freeze to death during the night," Serena said.

"No, he won't," Gus replied. "He's got a heavy coat. Dogs don't freeze like people do. He'll find some place to keep warm."

"Oh, Gus!" she cried. "He can't find a place! Don't you hear him? He's in a fox trap! I can tell. Listen!"

At that moment, they heard a long, drawn-out bark, thin and high as though it came from miles away.

"Well, there's nothing we can do," Gus said, wondering how long he could prolong Serena's stay in the blue room. Standing there in the blanket she made the room seem almost ordinary, as if it were daytime. What if he told her how afraid he was to be up there by himself on the third floor? She wouldn't snort like Zack would, or say something dumb like Rachel. She would probably offer to stay with him, curl herself up in her blanket on the floor like a caterpillar. Then he would go around for days feeling ashamed of himself but looking stony. He sighed.

"There is something we can do," Serena said. "We can go and find him."

"We cannot," he said.

"We could take Sheltie," she said.

"You know Sheltie won't hardly go three feet from the door when it's cold and dark outside," he said in a cranky voice.

"And we can take a sandwich for when we get hungry. And some dog biscuits for Tipper." She had stopped crying now and had that special look on her face, the expression she always got when she was planning something.

"Momma wouldn't let you go," he said.

"But we can't leave him out there all night!" She started to cry again. "Just listen to him! All by himself in the forest somewhere!"

"Oh, Serena," he cried. "There aren't enough trees on those hills to make even a little forest. Anyhow, somebody over there across the meadow will hear him. They'll go get him."

"No, they won't," she wailed.

That dog hated him. He didn't like that dog. How could he possibly go out into the dark after it?

"It's beginning to snow," he said, looking at the windows.

"Oh!" she sobbed.

He could see himself, a little speck, walking across those empty fields, up those black ridges.

"We could wake up Poppa and ask him to go find Tipper," he said hopelessly.

She looked at him with an expression that was almost angry.

"You know he wouldn't go," she said. He did know it. There were certain things you couldn't ask parents about at all. Poppa would be annoyed with them for waking him up about that stray old dog. Then he would smooth everything down, talking, talking, until it got to be unimportant.

"I'll go a little way," he said.

She smiled instantly. "Oh, Gus, I knew you would," she said. Then she marched over to his cot and threw her arms around his neck and hugged him.

Gus didn't smile. He didn't frown. And when Serena stood back, he wiped her tears off his neck and put his feet down on the floor, noting that his white socks were already gray socks. Suddenly he remembered how he used to tie Serena's shoe laces. Now she tied Simon's. Someday soon Simon would learn to tie his own. It was almost funny to think that, long ago, Zack must have come into Gus's room every morning and tied *his* shoe laces.

"How will I get my jacket?" he wondered aloud as he picked up the geode. "I don't want to wake Great-aunt Hattie."

"I can be as quiet as a shadow," promised Serena. "I'll get it."

They crept down the stairs. Leaving the blue room was like being rescued from a locked closet. Nothing could be worse than that, Gus thought, not thinking too hard about what was ahead of him.

When they got to his room, they saw a little yellow line of light shining between the bottom of the door and the floor. They looked at each other.

"What'll we do?" whispered Gus.

They heard Sheltie padding behind them in the hall. He must be going to his usual place next to the radiator. "I haven't heard your dog yipping," Gus added.

"I have," Serena whispered back. "Listen!"

Serena must be imagining things now, Gus thought. He couldn't hear a thing except their breathing.

"I can't go out without my jacket and hat and gloves," he said.

Serena knocked on the door.

"Come in," said Great-aunt Hattie. They opened the door. She was sitting at Gus's desk, turning the pages of a book. He was surprised to see she was looking at his geography.

"Everything is in the wrong place," said Great-aunt Hattie.

"We have to get something," Serena said.

"Help yourself," said Great-aunt Hattie, looking thoughtfully at Gus. He wished she wouldn't stare at him so. He picked up his jacket from the floor, dug his mittens and hat out of the closet and found an old scarf of Zack's underneath some shoes.

"Going somewhere?" asked Great-aunt Hattie.

"I just remembered I left something outside," muttered Gus.

"It's two o'clock in the morning," observed the old lady. "But memory strikes at all hours."

Then she picked up her blue pocketbook that was lying, as usual, on her feet. She dug around for a minute, then produced a pair of green woolly earmuffs.

"You might like to wear these beneath your cap. It's extremely cold outdoors. I don't know how you people survive in these northern climes. Here." And she held them out. Gus took them without any intention of using them. He hated earmuffs.

Then he got his clothes and piled them all up over his arm. He and Serena left Great-aunt Hattie to her reading. She didn't look up as they left the room.

After Gus had dressed, he and Serena went down to the kitchen. Serena made him a lumpy peanut-butter sandwich and wrapped it in waxed paper.

"It'll be too cold to eat," he said.

She gave him a handful of dog biscuits.

"I'll never be able to find that dog," he said.

Serena opened the door to the summer kitchen. "I'll get your boots," she said.

"I'll get them," he said roughly.

He found them next to a sled and pulled them over his shoes. Serena wrapped herself up tightly in the blanket and stood in the open doorway to watch him leave.

"I'll get lost in the dark," he said.

"I'll wait up for you," said Serena.

"Momma will wake up and see the light and then we'll get it," said Gus.

"Then I'll wait in my room with the light off," said Serena.

He felt around in his jacket pocket for a mitten

and his fingers encountered the geode. He must have dropped it in the pocket without thinking about it. That dumb stone!

And the well! He'd forgotten about that. He hesitated. He knew it was somewhere in the orchard. But exactly where? He'd always been too scared to go right up to it. Oh, it was cold! He pulled Zack's scarf around his chin.

"Serena, I can't go," he said.

The dog's cry echoed around them. It sounded weaker than it had before. Oh, why didn't the dog give up!

"Please," begged Serena, huddled in her blanket.

He stepped off the back step into the snow.

"Maybe Great-aunt Hattie will wake Poppa and tell him I've gone outside," he said.

"She won't tell," Serena said. "I know she won't."

"You do not!" Gus shouted. Serena looked stricken. She held up a finger to her mouth. "You'll wake them," she said urgently.

He took a few steps, then looked back. Serena's feet stuck out beneath the blanket. The snow was falling softly. It wasn't a heavy fall, just dots of cold touching his nose and forehead and cheeks. Then

slowly the kitchen door was shut. He watched Serena through the kitchen windows. She was covering the jar of peanut butter. Then she turned out the kitchen light. Now the house was dark unless Great-aunt Hattie was still awake in his room on the other side.

He looked straight up to the windows of the blue room. He could barely make them out. But had something moved behind them? Did something swim there behind the black glass, and had he glimpsed it, like a fish seen briefly in muddy water?

Why hadn't Serena waked Zack who was older and who didn't imagine things and who went through a door as if he were knocking it down? But Gus knew the answer to his own question. Zack would have rolled over in bed and told Serena to leave him alone.

Rachel asked favors from Zack, and Serena asked favors from him. Only Simon seemed to stand alone. But Simon wasn't quite alone. He had his broom and he had Momma. Well, Gus supposed they all had Momma and Poppa, but in different ways.

There was an empty milk bottle leaning at an angle near the step. As the snow flakes struck it there were tiny clicks. Near it was the rusted handle of an old red wagon of Simon's, sticking up out of a drift. Both the handle and the bottle were pointing toward the door. He felt they were directing him to go back inside, like messages in a treasure hunt. Only a few feet away, and he would be in the wilderness of the orchard, of the snow drifts, beyond the places where Simon would leave a wagon, or his mother would forget a milk bottle.

If he just went as far as the edge of the orchard, where the last and oldest apple trees stood, and then turned right around and came back, how would Serena know? He could stay outside the kitchen door for a little while, then go in and tell her he hadn't been able to find Tipper. Or he could sit in Great-aunt Hattie's car. It looked enormous there in the dark.

Gus felt clever, and ashamed, at the thought of the fib he could tell Serena. It wouldn't be a serious fib, like saying you hadn't done something when you had, or blaming someone else for what you did. And everyone made up stories, especially Rachel. Even Serena made up things about her animals. And he *would start*, at least, to search for the dog.

Holding on to the car, he made his way around it and across the drive. Each step he took broke through the crust of the old snow upon which a new powdery layer was already forming. In the cold and cottoned silence, the sky seemed to have been lowered so that it hung just over his head. He could see ahead the snow lying along the crooked, root-like branches of the apple trees, emitting a pale radiance as mysterious as that which came from the geode.

Gus dug his boots into the little rise on the other side of the drive and scrambled up until he was on top.

chapter 6

He looked back once more at the house. It was nothing but a dark shape. If he shouted, would the lights go on in room after room? Would it become a house again, then?

The dog howled. Even though he knew the dog was far away, the sound was as clear as if Tipper were standing only a few feet from him, watching him, laughing at him. Not that dogs really laughed. The howl died away in a series of small sharp yelps.

From behind Gus, a light wind came and blew a shower of snow across his neck. The sound of the wind was like a great sigh, or a softly spoken word he could not quite make out.

The apple trees were old and twisted and they had been planted long before the Olivers lived in the house. Mr. Oliver was always saying he ought to prune and spray them, but he never got around to it. So the apples were knotty with bumps, and wormy. But sometimes Gus found one on the ground, warmed by the sun, with all the sweetness of the fruit gathered into one place. Once Rachel had asked him what was worse than finding a worm in an apple you were eating. He hadn't known the answer. "Half a worm!" she had shouted and screeched with laughter.

In the spring, the blue jays would be hopping all over the branches, bombarding Serena's stray cats when they climbed the trees to get at the jays' eggs. Now the trees were deserted, without apples or birds or cats.

A few feet ahead, he could make out a clearing. That was where the well was, wasn't it? He stood still. It was like balancing on the edge of a cliff. Now would be a good time to turn around and go back. In the morning, everything would be as usual. Except for Great-aunt Hattie. But then, she had said she was leaving at the crack of dawn. He imagined himself going to school, trudging through the snow to the bus, keeping one eye on Serena's red boots nearby. The boys in his class would try to make him laugh before the bell rang, just as they did every morning. The girls would giggle because he wouldn't laugh. The teacher would say, "Good morning, children," and that would be that. He wished he wasn't always imagining what was going to happen.

His ears hurt. He took out the green muffs and placed them on his ears. They felt awful, like two fuzzy hands clapped to either ear. He'd better keep moving. He jumped up and down until he was out of breath. Then, staring at the clearing ahead, he heard once again, right through the ear muffs, the howl of the dog. Serena would hear it too.

He was comforted suddenly, thinking of her in her room, looking out the window probably, thinking about him perhaps. It was as though the end of a strong rope had been placed in his hand, the other end of which Serena held.

"Walk!" he commanded himself.

After all, didn't he know every stone and slope and field and tree around? Just because it was dark and snowy and late, all of that didn't change the way things were. He walked into the clearing.

The dark and the snow and the lateness of the hour *did* change things. This did not look like a place he had ever been, ever seen. The pine trees in a small stand on the other side of the clearing were separate brooding figures, their boughs bent down with snow, like arms pointing at the ground. Over the ground the snow made little hills and valleys, frozen into luminous waves. In the exact center of the clearing, between the apple trees and the pines, a board slanted out of the snow. It must be the well. The board was splintered with a ragged edge that caught and held the snow.

Gus stared at the dreadful place. He took off the ear muffs and strained to listen. There was nothing but the snow falling. What happened to the milk snakes in the winter? Were they curled up just beneath the boarded well cover? Asleep among the dank stones? Was the snow seeping into the well, filling it up?

He felt he had lost touch with Serena. She wasn't afraid of the well. She didn't know what it was like to be afraid. He took a cautious step back, then another, then veered off down the slope of the hill toward the road below. But midway down, he turned abruptly and went back up, following the pockets his footprints had left in the snow.

Once more in the clearing, he inched closer to the

board, out of breath with excitement, not knowing why he was doing what he was doing. He reached out until his mittened hand took hold of the piece of wood, then he yanked at it. There was a loud creak and the board came loose in his hand. He stepped back and stuck the board upright in the exact place he had been standing. Now he had marked it. In the morning, he would be able to see his marker, know that he had been there. He felt like smiling. Surely, he could smile out here in the dark, where there was no one around to see him. He took off his mitten and touched his mouth. It was not smiling.

The dog howled. Gus went back down the slope to the road. The falling snow made the dog's howl a pool of sound all around Gus. It was as though each flake carried a bit of that yelp. He stood on the road and thought. There was an old man who lived in a house on the opposite ridge, across the road and the meadows. It was said he set out traps to catch foxes. It was said that sometimes the old man even caught a fox, killed it and sold the pelt to someone who drove all around the villages in that section of the country, visiting the old men who had once been farmers and who mostly lived by themselves in their old gray

75

houses, buying their pelts and selling them in the city.

Gus had seen that house on his way to school, had seen a thin spiral of smoke coming out of the chimney. He would try there first. If the dog wasn't there, he'd come home. Mr. Oliver had warned the children to be careful about the deep snow; he had told them not to go up the ridge. Traps could be hidden in drifts and some of them were cruel, catching a creature around its legs so it couldn't pull free. If Tipper were caught in such a trap, Gus wondered how he would ever pry him loose. He had seen such a trap once, all rusted, with sharp pointed teeth like those in the jaws of an alligator.

There were no footprints on the road except Gus's own. He went down into the little ditch on the side of the road and up the other side to the stone wall. As he clutched at the stones, one came loose and thudded thickly to the ground. After he was over and in the meadow, he found that his mittens were soaked. His fingers were cold and wet. He thrust his hands into the pockets of his jacket. The peanut-butter sandwich! He munched it, walking through the meadow. The peanut butter was half frozen, but still it tasted good and it reminded him of the kitchen and the cluttered shelves where all the jars of jam and jelly were kept.

The wind blew hard across the field. There were no trees to make a windbreak. The snow fell steadily. It was difficult to walk now. He had to lift his feet way up in the air, and each time he did, his boots were laden with snow. Ahead of him, past an abandoned shed, loomed the ridge. Serena had found an old iron in that shed, and Mrs. Oliver had said it was the kind people used before they had electricity, when they had to heat up irons on their stoves. Serena used it to hold her door open in the summer when all the breezes of the valley blew through the Oliver house and kept the doors banging to and fro and the curtains flying at the windows. He had never explored the shed because Serena told him it was full of wasps.

All at once he realized the snow had stopped as suddenly as it had begun. There was no longer the sound of the snowflakes, and the wind dropped so that he could hear his feet breaking through the crust, making a noise like cotton tearing, and he thought of his mother tearing up old sheets to make cleaning rags.

He paused near the shed. If only the dog were inside it. Then all he would have to do would be to yank open the old wooden door and the dog could run home ahead of him. If Serena had been with him, the dog would probably have been in the shed. What happened in Gus's imagination seemed to happen in real life to Serena.

He knew the dog wasn't there, but he wanted to look inside. He kicked the snow away from the door and after straining and pulling, managed to get it half open. He poked his head in. It was black and silent inside. He was sure that above, suspended from the rafters of the roof, the gray wasps' nests hung like lanterns. Something squeaked, something moved.

Gus jumped back, clipping his head on the edge of the door. The sharp bang echoed all about him, bounced off the blackness of the sky, the frozen whiteness of the meadow. He listened, standing just outside the shed, his hand pressed against the bump on his head. The silence came back all at once and with it, Gus began to feel a new kind of cold, one that seemed lodged inside him like a large splinter of ice, so that each breath he took was like a bucket of ice water drawn from the well.

78

The dog had been quiet for so long that now, when its cry came to him again from somewhere up the ridge, he was startled and had to think all over again about what he had to do. It was hard to move away from the shed. Even though he did not care to think about what was inside it, it was a kind of house.

He reached the stone wall on the other side of the meadow. Beyond it, the ground began to rise abruptly. The leafless branches of oaks and vines coiled like springs above the snow. He had told Serena there was no forest on the ridge, but standing there, hesitating to go on, he saw that he had been wrong. Above him, the pines appeared impenetrable, massed like a silent army on the slope. He turned around to look back.

There, across the meadow and the road, beyond the shed and up the hill was *his* house. But was it his house? Why, it was no more than a shadow on the hill!

For no reason he could think of, he suddenly opened his mouth and shouted, "Gus!"

He must keep moving. It was getting hard to tell where his feet were. He trudged along the side of the rise and then suddenly he saw animal tracks, four

black marks in the snow. If Zack had been with him, Zack would have known what animal had made them.

The tracks led straight up the ridge. If they were the dog's and the dog had gotten through the pines, then he could too. But what if they weren't the dog's? He began to climb, fell forward, scratched his nose on a branch, caught hold of a tree trunk, got a new load of snow in his boots, lost his hat, retrieved it, and found himself all at once among the pine trees.

Here there were patches of bare ground and a vague damp smell of earth. It seemed somewhat less cold. He shook the snow from his boots and blew on his frozen fingers. He had not known there were so many different kinds of silence, nor that silence could be so loud, could ring like a bell as it had on the meadow, or that it could, as it did here, have a kind of roar in it.

The tracks had disappeared; the earth was too hard to take imprints. He began to run, his hands held out in front of him to ward off the branches which thrust out from the trees. Then, unexpectedly, he emerged into a clearing. He was out of breath. He stood for a moment looking up. The slope had leveled out a

little and before him there was a round meadow like
a white saucer slightly tipped, and at its other end,
another line of pines. At the very top of the meadow,
he saw the dog.

It was standing on three of its legs but the fourth
was bent beneath its body.

Gus felt dizzy. He felt that he had burst into tears.
But there were no tears on his face. To make sure, he
felt his cheeks. Then he began to run through the
snow toward the dog. The dog whimpered and cried
and tried to run, hopping frantically on its three legs.
The dog's tail was curled beneath it. Its head circled
wildly. The meadow was full of noise, as of flocks of
birds flapping their wings and rising from the ground.
Gus's breath came through his mouth, sharp and
whistling and the dog thrashed about and cried. The
animal seemed to have gone mad. Even as he was rushing toward it, Gus wondered how he would ever get
close to the trap. If the dog would only sit down for a
second, be still, be calm, be friendly.

"Stop it!" Gus shouted, running around the dog,
seeing the trap now, its circling teeth holding the animal's paw.

"*You stop it!*" thundered a voice from above.

82

Gus stopped in his tracks. Emerging from the woods was a tall man wrapped up like a package, a rifle slung across one shoulder. Only the man's eyes were visible above the ragged scarf that circled around and around his head.

chapter 7

For a second Gus thought the man intended to shoot the dog. But no, he had only unslung the rifle from his shoulder.

"That's my dog," Gus said. His own voice sounded peculiar, as though it were melting away like an ice cube in the sink. Tipper crouched and cried.

"It's my fox," said the man.

"But it's not a fox!" Gus cried.

"Maybe not, but it's got a good coat," said the man peering down at the animal.

"No, no," protested Gus. "It's just an old dog, an old stray dog my sister found."

"Maybe so," replied the man. "But whatever it is, it belongs to me. This is my land you're standing on."

"I didn't know it was yours," said Gus.

"You know now." The man bent over the trap. He muttered to himself. Then there was a sharp crack like a shot. A minute later, Tipper limped away, freed, and began to lick his paw.

"You let him loose," said Gus.

"You think I don't know a dog when I see one?" asked the man. He pulled the scarf down from his chin, revealing a scraggly white beard. Gus saw that he was old.

"Can I take him home?" Gus asked.

"Where's that?" asked the old man. He didn't wait for an answer but bent over Tipper. "His leg's not broken," he said. "But it's going to be sore for a while."

"Over there," Gus answered, waving his arm. "That house on the other ridge."

"If he weren't such an old dog, I'd keep him," said the man. "What gets caught on my land belongs to me."

Gus waited. The man had his own ideas.

"But, since he's just an old dog, I suppose you can take him. I don't see him running up to greet you like any natural dog would. How do I know he's yours?"

"We just found him today," Gus said, thinking to

himself that it felt like years since Serena had scrambled over the wall to go and get the dog. "He doesn't know me yet," he added. It was a certain kind of lie. If the dog had known him all his life, it still wouldn't have run to him.

"Is that a fact?" said the old man. "Guess he doesn't much care for your hospitality, running off and leaving you like that."

Gus couldn't think of anything to answer. His feet were going numb again because he had been standing in one spot for so long. As unobtrusively as he could, he began to jump back and forth on one foot, then the other.

"You'd never have sprung that trap by yourself," said the old man. "You're lucky I don't hardly sleep at night. When I do sleep, I don't hear anything. I wouldn't hear the end of the world when it came."

What would the end of the world sound like? Gus wondered fleetingly. Rachel would probably know. "Well, I'll go now," Gus said, taking a step toward Tipper. To his intense chagrin, he heard a low growl. What was the *matter* with that dumb creature! Didn't he *know* what Gus had done for him? He hoped the man hadn't heard that growl.

"You'd best come home with me first and stay in the warm for a bit. It's a long way back in this cold. Hurry up now, don't argue. Just come along and bring the dog," said the old man.

Gus hadn't thought of arguing. He was afraid Tipper wouldn't even follow him home. He'd need a rope probably. He'd have to drag him through the snow like a balky cow. Gus felt utterly discouraged.

"Come on, dog," the old man called over his shoulder, and Tipper got up and followed, limping.

On the other side of the pines there was a clearing, and in the clearing a small old house. It leaned to one side as though the wind had pushed it so. A thin line of smoke rose straight up from the chimney. There was a light on inside the house, a flickering light like that made by a candle or a small fire. The window was smoky.

"Stamp the snow off your boots," said the old man. "The house is cold and damp enough."

When Gus stepped through the door that the old man was holding open for him, he found himself in a small room so cluttered with objects that it looked like the Oliver attic. A kerosene lamp burned on a rectangular wooden table, its yellow light revealing bowls and pots, cans of food, plates and cutlery, a hand ax, a hammer, a box of buttons and some old newspapers. There was a fireplace but in it, instead of burning logs, was a small stout black stove, its pipe disappearing up the chimney. There were chairs everywhere, broken chairs, old chairs, chairs covered with faded flat pillows or strips of dark cloth, and on the seat of one of them a pair of highbuttoned black shoes of the kind Gus had seen only in pictures. There were boxes on the floor, cardboard boxes, wooden boxes and a dented metal box on which were painted flowers and birds. There were calendars tacked to the wall or hanging from nails by string, old calendars with bright pictures of gardens, waterfalls, streams winding through woods and cows standing in light green meadows. A huge scarred chest of drawers leaned from the wall as though about to topple over. Underneath one of its thick claw feet, someone had wedged a piece of wood. Then Gus saw how the floor sloped and rose as if moles had worked their passages beneath it. On top of the chest were photographs glued to cardboard stands. In their midst stood a big clock with Roman numerals. It had a double tick like the Oliver alarm clock and it said four o'clock.

In the morning? Gus wondered. And he felt a flash of excitement at being awake and away from home at such an extraordinary hour.

There were coat hooks on the wall and from them hung dark garments with long drooping sleeves. On one of these hooks the old man hung the gun. On top of the stove, a kettle steamed. Then something jumped at Gus's leg. It was a small cat that looked as if it had been dipped in orange juice. The cat looked up at him and mewed. One of its eyes was strange, a white marble.

"Old cat," remarked the man. "Blind in one eye. We found her out in the woods too."

We?

Gus turned back to the stove. Next to it was a rocking chair he had not yet noticed and in it was an old, old woman, very small, like a doll. She was staring at the red line of heat which circled the door of the stove. She was very still, not rocking, just lying back in the chair.

"Now we'll have a cup of tea and that will warm you. And I suppose you'll need a rope for that old dog since he doesn't appear to care for you much," the old man said, showing he *had* heard Tipper growl.

Gus was embarrassed. He looked at Tipper who was huddled in a corner watching the cat which ignored him. Gus nodded at the old man. He looked back at the old woman.

"We don't sleep much," the man said. "Old people don't, you know. She and I, we like the nighttime. We go through our things in those boxes. We read old letters—even the bills can be interesting, although I never used to think so when I was paying them. We look at our photographs and calendars. I used to write things down on the calendars, things that we did or that happened to us. We find those dates and we talk about those old times. Then we have our tea and a biscuit or two. It's not so bad."

The old lady turned her head slowly and looked at Gus. She smiled. She had very few teeth.

"She's spry, you know," said the old man, setting out three cups on the table next to a brown tea pot with a chipped nozzle. He opened a tin canister and shook it. "Getting low on tea," he said. "Did you hear me, Lydia?"

The old lady nodded and laughed. She had a light, free laugh and to Gus's surprise the sound reminded him of Serena. But Serena would never get so old. How could anyone live so long?

91

"Soon I'll have to go to town and get us some supplies," the man said. The old lady laughed again as though he had told her a joke.

"Now show this boy how spry you are," the old man said. The old lady rocked the chair forward until her small black-shod feet touched the floor. She was wearing a long black dress and when she stood up, it rustled. It must be taffeta, like Rachel's party dress. She made a strange little jump and then, holding her skirt out with her two hands, she did a little dance in front of the stove, smiling, wobbling slightly, kicking one foot out, then the other. Then she fell back softly into the rocker like a feather coming to rest.

The old man had made the tea. He handed Gus a steaming cup.

"Drink it all down," he said. "It'll keep you upright until you get home. Now, let me find a rope for the dog." He began to look in boxes and behind chairs. "There!" he said at last, and held up a length of washline. "This will do."

"Hobby," said the old lady suddenly. "You must mark it down on the calendar about our visitor tonight."

"Good idea," said the old man, drinking his tea standing up.

"My tea," said the old lady.

"Oh, yes. I forgot," said the man and he put a cup on a saucer that didn't match and handed it to her.

"What a treat," she said.

The three of them drank their tea, the old man blowing on his and gurgling a little as it went down. But the old lady drank in small sips, holding the cup delicately with two fingers.

"I know your house," said the old man. "It used to belong to the Carters. He was a real farmer. All those fields used to belong to him. There's quite a few of you, isn't there? I see little children out there on the slope."

"Five," Gus said. "I've got two brothers and two sisters."

"I had ten," said the old man. "Six brothers and four sisters. I liked a few of them quite well. Lydia was an only child. We often envy each other."

"There's a blue room in the house," Gus said suddenly. "It's all painted bright blue." A *mean* blue, he thought privately.

"Is there now?" said the man. "That's a flighty color to paint a room. I don't think Carter would have done that, do you, Lydia? Who was it owned the house before the Carters?"

Lydia put down her cup on a stool and took her thin old chin between her two fingers. "The Howells," she replied. "And before them, the Gerows. And before that, I don't recall."

So many people had lived in the Oliver house! It didn't seem possible. Where had they all gone? What had become of them?

The old lady dozed. Gus picked up the rope from the table where the old man had neatly coiled it.

"I'll tie it around the dog's neck," said the man. "It needs a special kind of knot."

Gus wrapped his scarf around his face and buttoned up his jacket. His mittens felt like frogs. The old man straightened up from where he had been leaning over the dog, then put the end of the rope in Gus's hand.

"You don't say much, do you," he observed.

Gus felt a wild flare-up of words in his head, but they staggered and stuttered and then fell into fragments. He said, "Thank you for the tea."

The old man nodded. "Don't mention it," he said.

"Very much," Gus managed to add.

"Have a good journey," chirped the old lady unexpectedly.

Gus waved a limp mitten at her and, leading the dog, went out the door. It closed definitely behind him.

He looked back once. The glow of the kerosene lamp shone out of the dark mass of the little house. Gus felt in his pocket for the stone Great-aunt Hattie had given him. It was still there, a dark dull little stone with its own glow.

It seemed to take much less time to go through the upper field, down among the pines and over the stone wall than it had to get up. Tipper limped along behind him. At least he wasn't growling now. Gus wasn't scared of the night the way he had been— Tipper was company even if he wasn't good company—but he was tired to his bones and the warming effect of the tea had worn off almost as soon as the door had closed behind him.

The big meadow at the bottom of the ridge seemed to have grown twice as large as it had been when he crossed it earlier. Gus saw his tracks in the snow; he saw the shed door where he had stood. How curious the passing of time was. He had thought he would never get up the ridge, never find the dog. Now that was all past. In the morning, on the way to school, if it didn't snow again, he would be able to see his tracks going and returning. This very moment of coldness and weariness would have passed. The tracks would be the only trace left of what had really happened to him.

Gus felt, rather than saw, a change in the light. It was very slight, but it was there. Although the clumps of trees and the shed and stone walls still made dense shadows, there was a kind of grayness in the air as though the black had been diluted. Tipper slipped and skidded, regained his balance and limped after him.

Looking ahead, Gus could make out the windows of home, the horizontal lines of the clapboard siding and the drain pipe which outlined the roof. The night was slipping away, leaving behind it the familiar, ordinary daytime things.

When they came to the last stone wall, Tipper needed help to get over. All the time that Gus was lifting him and pushing him, the dog growled. Gus felt hopeless. Nobody appreciated anything. "You creep," he said to the dog and felt a little better.

They climbed the driveway which led up the hill to the kitchen door. Gus would have liked to have lain down right there on the snow. He imagined what might happen. The dog would sit next to him, frozen solid but loyal to the end. Someone would see him from the house and then everyone would run out, shouting and horrified!

How they would regret the way they had treated him! As a tribute, Simon would bury his broom in the ground, digging a hole with his bare hands. Rachel would think of all the Turkish Delight she had not given him. Zack would remember all the times he had called Gus stupid. But then, he thought disgustedly, he wouldn't be able to see how ashamed they were because he would be frozen solid too.

And, then, there was Serena. Serena would really cry. He didn't have much to reproach her with. Although she *had* made him go out and find the dog. How had she gotten him to do it? And he had hardly argued with her.

chapter 8

Gus edged between the corner of the house and Great-aunt Hattie's Stutz Bearcat. He was back where he had started from.

But it was no longer dark. Upon the milk bottle now nearly filled with snow, the handle of Simon's wagon and his own footprints leading out to the orchard, fell the yellow reflection of the kitchen light. And when he looked through the window, he saw that not only was the kitchen light on, but that everyone except Zack was there.

Gus felt breathless. Had Serena awakened them all to tell them where he had gone? Were they furious with him? Were they alarmed? Worried?

Shivering with cold now, he stared through the window at his family. They didn't *look* furious or alarmed. Great-aunt Hattie was sitting at the table drinking coffee, the silver flask beside her cup. Mr. and Mrs. Oliver were standing nearby, speaking to her. Simon was eating a banana. Rachel was plastering a slice of bread with raspberry jam. Serena was building a little house with sugar cubes. They all looked so *complete*.

Then Zack walked in through the door playing catch with a sneaker. Gus saw Mr. Oliver turn and say something to Zack. Then Zack dropped the sneaker.

Perhaps he ought never to go back, Gus thought. But even as the thought drifted through his mind, he was opening the back door, pulling off his water-logged boots and untying the knot around Tipper's neck.

He walked into the kitchen.

Silence.

Then Serena ran toward the dog and buried her face in his neck fur.

"Why, hello, Gus," said Mr. Oliver.

Mrs. Oliver smiled at him. "I knew you'd find him," she said. "Where was he? Just up the ridge? Get those wet clothes off and I'll make you breakfast."

"Where on earth did you put the alarm clock?"

asked his father. "We've been looking all over the house for it."

"You're dripping on my bare foot," exclaimed Zack.

"Ugh!" cried Rachel. "You've got a big scratch on your nose."

Simon snatched his broom from under the kitchen table and with a joyous face prepared to swing at Gus.

"Dum-dum sneaked out in the middle of the night!" he shouted.

In one swift movement, Gus took hold of Simon's pajama-covered ankles and lifted him up until he was hanging upside down, his head a foot off the floor. The broom fell out of Simon's hands with a clatter.

"I will never let you go," said Gus, his own voice louder than anything he had ever heard. "We'll stay like this forever and ever until you *promise*—" But he was going to burst! He couldn't say another word. He held on to Simon's ankles, they were both statues now, imprisoned in stone, silent as stone. Everyone was watching, even Great-aunt Hattie. No one spoke.

Then, as from a great distance, Gus heard Simon say, "I promise. I promise." And Gus lowered him slowly to the floor.

Great-aunt Hattie stood up, holding on to her blue pocketbook.

"You've had a long journey," she said briskly to Gus. "But you arrived back home in time to say goodbye to me. I'm off to warmer climes and sunny skies."

Someone pressed a warm cup of cocoa into Gus's hand. Simon picked up his banana and finished it, staring thoughtfully at his broom on the floor. Zack sat down and put on his other sneaker. Rachel cracked eggs into a brown bowl. Serena fed Tipper dog biscuits. Mr. Oliver went off to shave. Mrs. Oliver sliced bread for toast.

Gus drank his cocoa and went to his room to change his clothes. Except for the geography book open on his desk, everything was the same. Then he turned to his window. Great-aunt Hattie was standing in front of it, watching him silently.

"I hope the ear muffs were of use," she said.

"Thank you," he said.

"Keep them as a momento of your journey," she said as Gus held them out to her.

"I got very cold," he said, feeling he had to say something.

"You must have been fearfully cold," she said.

"You must have been scared. How many times did you think of simply turning around and coming home and making up a story for Serena?"

Gus's face grew warm. He would liked to have made a hideous face at her. It was dreadful, the way she looked inside his head. Yet, at the same time, he felt like laughing. But *she* was laughing! Suddenly she placed a thumb in each of her ears and flapped her fingers at him.

"Oh!" he exclaimed and clapped a hand over his mouth. His head was bursting with laughter! All at once, she looked at him gravely.

"But you didn't come back without the dog. You didn't make up a story for Serena. Don't forget it. I won't."

Then she walked quickly from his room. Her voice came back like a scarf trailing behind her. "These doors make me melancholy," he heard her say.

When he returned to the kitchen, Great-aunt Hattie was dressed in her tweed coat, standing by the back door. She was speaking to Serena.

"Unless you want that animal exceedingly," she was saying, "I'll take him with me back to Italy.

He'll do well there. He can warm his old bones in the sunlight."

"Well, I like him," Serena said.

"That doesn't mean you have to keep him," replied Great-aunt Hattie. Serena hesitated a long time. Then Tipper limped over to Great-aunt Hattie and sat down next to her.

"All right," Serena said at last.

Great-aunt Hattie opened her blue pocketbook and after rummaging around for a minute produced a collar and a bright red dog leash the same color as the Stutz Bearcat.

"Imagine carrying around a leash without a dog," she said, giving voice to Gus's unspoken thought.

"Goodbye," said everyone, including Mr. Oliver who had come back to the kitchen with his shiny after-shaving face. "Good trip! Good luck!" everyone said.

They watched through the kitchen window. There was a long unearthly growl as Great-aunt Hattie started up the motor. Tipper was sitting next to her on the front seat looking lively.

Then the children all ran to the living room so they could watch Great-aunt Hattie drive along the snow-covered road down the hill in front of the house.

Gus pressed his nose against the chilled window pane. It was light out now. From the eastern sky, an extraordinary radiance emanated from three red lines that stretched along the sky as far as he could see. Looking down at the road, he saw the red car gathering speed. The red light touched it. It seemed for an instant to be made out of dust, a streak of red dust traveling along the ground. Then the car disappeared around the farthest corner.

"Crazy old lady," said Zack.

"She probably came to announce the end of the world," said Rachel with her silly giggle.

"She was probably a witch," murmured Serena.

Simon just laughed.

Gus said nothing. He took the geode from his pocket where he had transferred it from his jacket. It gleamed as he held it up to the window where it caught the rays from the rising sun.

"Hey," cried Zack. "Let's break open the stone and see what's inside."

"No," said Gus.

Serena took hold of Gus's hand that held the stone

and brought it up until it was close to her right eye. She squinted a little. "It's like a crystal palace," she said wonderingly.

"Oh, come on, Gus," Zack said. "Don't be such a creep. I'll go get the hammer."

"No," Gus said again. He put the stone away in his pocket.

He knew how the stone would look inside, but he didn't choose to break it open yet. When he felt like it, he would take the hammer and tap the geode in such a way that it would break perfectly, in such a way that not one of the crystals inside would be broken.

But until then, until he wanted to, no one would touch it.